THE
SQUEEZE-MORE-INN

Elizabeth Ferber

Scholastic Canada Ltd.

To my mother.

Scholastic Canada Ltd.
123 Newkirk Road, Richmond Hill, Ontario, Canada L4C 3G5

Scholastic Inc.
555 Broadway, New York, NY 10012, USA

Ashton Scholastic Limited
Private Bag 92801, Penrose, Auckland, New Zealand

Ashton Scholastic Pty Limited
PO Box 579, Gosford, NSW 2250, Australia

Scholastic Publications Ltd.
Villiers House, Clarendon Avenue, Leamington Spa
Warwickshire CV32 5PR, UK

Canadian Cataloguing in Publication Data

Ferber, Elizabeth, 1953-
   The Squeeze More Inn

ISBN 0-590-24444-2

I. Title.

PS8561.E65S68 1995   jC813'.54   C95-930000-7
PZ7.F47S68 1995

6 5 4 3 2 1   Printed in Canada   5 6 7 8 9/9

I had a best friend named Maureen.

Every summer, Maureen and her parents went to their cottage. They called it "The Squeeze-More-Inn."

4

One weekend, they invited me to come along.
We left early in the morning.

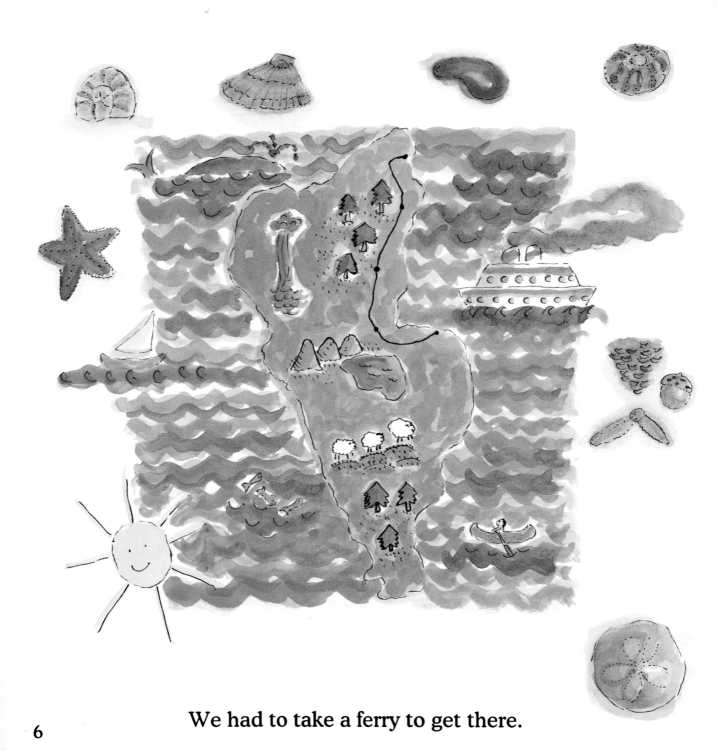

We had to take a ferry to get there.

Then we drove up a long, winding road.

As soon as we arrived we put on our bathing suits and ran down to the beach.

8

We played there for hours, collecting shells . . .

building a sandcastle . . .

Then we had a picnic while the hot sun dried our salty skin.

In the afternoon we picked berries. We ate so many our tongues turned blue.

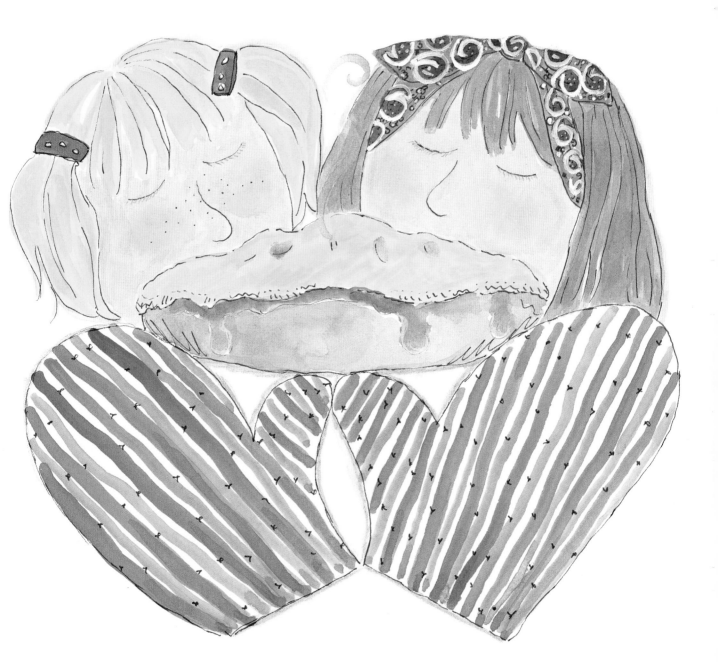

There were just enough berries left for Maureen's dad
to bake us a big juicy pie.

At night we had a huge bonfire and roasted wieners.

The moon was gigantic and there were a million tiny stars.

We got stomachaches from laughing so hard.
We tried to stay awake, but the next thing we knew,
it was morning.

For breakfast I had four pieces of toast with honey and a glass of milk.

The best part of the whole weekend was when
we went fishing.

I caught my very first fish and Maureen's dad wrapped it in newspaper for me to take home.

23

After lunch we ran through the sprinkler . . .

made a fort . . .

fed the squirrels . . .

and watched frogs in the pond.

We took turns in the old tree swing
until it was time to go home.

We kept our shells, rocks and driftwood,

and put the crabs back in the ocean.

On the drive to the ferry we fell asleep in the back seat while Maureen's mom sang and her dad whistled just like a bird.

We watched from the ferry a long time as the island got smaller and smaller and finally disappeared.

I'll always remember that weekend at the
Squeeze-More-Inn and my best friend Maureen.